THE TWELVE DAYS OF WINTER

A School Counting Book

by Deborah Lee Rose

illustrated by Carey Armstrong-Ellis

SCHOLASTIC INC.

New York Toronto London Auckland Sydney
Mexico City New Delhi Hong Kong Buenos Aires

1 On the first day of winter, my teacher gave to me . . .

. . . a bird feeder in a snowy tree.

2 On the second day of winter,
my teacher gave to me
TWO teddy bears
and a bird feeder in a snowy tree.

3

On the third day of winter,
my teacher gave to me
THREE penguins,
two teddy bears,
and a bird feeder in a snowy tree.

On the fourth day of winter,
my teacher gave to me

4 FOUR weather words,

three penguins,
two teddy bears,
and a bird feeder in
a snowy tree.

Weekly Weather

Monday	snowy
Tuesday	windy
Wednesday	sunny
Thursday	

cloudy

S On the fifth day of winter,
my teacher gave to me
FIVE gold stars,
four weather words,
three penguins,
two teddy bears,
and a bird feeder in a snowy tree.

6 On the sixth day of winter,
my teacher gave to me
SIX socks for stuffing,

five gold stars,

four weather words,

three penguins,

two teddy bears,

and a bird feeder in a snowy tree.

7 On the seventh day of winter,
my teacher gave to me
SEVEN flakes for snipping,
six socks for stuffing,
five gold stars,
four weather words,
three penguins,
two teddy bears,
and a bird feeder in a snowy tree.

8

On the eighth day of winter,
my teacher gave to me
EIGHT bells for jingling,
seven flakes for snipping,
six socks for stuffing,
five gold stars,
four weather words,
three penguins,
two teddy bears,
and a bird feeder in a snowy tree.

9

On the ninth day of winter,
my teacher gave to me
NINE worms for watching,
eight bells for jingling,
seven flakes for snipping,
six socks for stuffing,
five gold stars,
four weather words,
three penguins,
two teddy bears,
and a bird feeder in
a snowy tree.

10

On the tenth day of winter,
my teacher gave to me
TEN holes for stitching,
nine worms for watching,
eight bells for jingling,
seven flakes for snipping,
six socks for stuffing,
five gold stars,
four weather words,
three penguins,
two teddy bears,
and a bird feeder in
a snowy tree.

Snow
snowman
snowball
snowflake
snowstorm
snow peas

11

On the eleventh day of winter,
my teacher gave to me
ELEVEN cubes for gluing,
ten holes for stitching,
nine worms for watching,
eight bells for jingling,
seven flakes for snipping,
six socks for stuffing,
five gold stars,
four weather words,
three penguins,
two teddy bears,
and a bird feeder in
a snowy tree.

12 On the twelfth day of winter, my teacher gave to me

TWELVE treats for tasting,

eleven cubes for gluing,

ten holes for stitching,

nine worms for watching,

eight bells for jingling,

seven flakes for snipping,

six socks for stuffing . . .

. . . five gold stars,
four weather words,
three penguins,
two teddy bears . . .

. . . and a bird feeder
in a snowy tree.

For all my school experts, big and small, and for Carey,

whose drawings made me want to see more of these characters' adventures —D. L. R.

To the co-op teachers at Coastal Ridge Elementary School —C. A-E.

ISBN-13: 978-0-545-11326-7
ISBN-10: 0-545-11326-1

Text copyright © 2006 by Deborah Lee Rose. Illustrations copyright © 2006 by Carey Armstrong-Ellis.
All rights reserved. Published by Scholastic Inc., 557 Broadway, New York, NY 10012.
by arrangement with Abrams Books for Young Readers, an imprint of Harry N. Abrams, Inc.
SCHOLASTIC and associated logos are trademarks and/or registered trademarks of Scholastic Inc.

12 11 10 9 8 7 6 5 4 3 2 1   8 9 10 11 12 13/0

Printed in the U.S.A.   08

This edition first printing, September 2008

Designed by Celina Carvalho